Words to Know Before You Read

Let's Learn The Digraph **Th** Sound

thermos
third
thirsty
thorn
thrill
thud
thumb
thump
thunder
Thursday

www.rourkeeducationalmedia.com

Edited by Precious McKenzie
Illustrated by Ed Myer
Art Direction, Cover and Page Layout by Tara Raymo

Library of Congress PCN Data

The Mountain Thrill / Meg Greve
ISBN 978-1-62169-266-9 (hard cover) (alk. paper)
ISBN 978-1-62169-224-9 (soft cover)
Library of Congress Control Number: 2012952771

Rourke Educational Media
Printed in the United States of America,
North Mankato, Minnesota

rourkeeducationalmedia.com

customerservice@rourkeeducationalmedia.com • PO Box 643328 Vero Beach, Florida 32964

The Mountain Thrill

Counselor
Gus

Counselor
Mindy

Fitz

Dex

Ana

Lizzie

Written By Meg Greve
Illustrated By Ed Myer

"Today is Thursday. Who wants to go hiking?" asks Counselor Gus.

"I'll get my boots!" says Lizzie.

"I'll get my thermos in case I get thirsty," says Dex.

"I want to go swimming," says Fitz.

"This way campers!" says Counselor Mindy.

"Everyone on the mountain tram!" calls Counselor Gus.

Lizzie hops on, then Ana jumps in. Dex is third and last is Fitz.

The tram stops in the middle of the trip.

"I think we should get out here," says Lizzie.

"That ride was a thrill!" says Ana.

"Where is the pool?" asks Fitz.

Dex leaps out with a THUD!

Next come the counselors.

The rest tumble out, one after the other.

THUMP! THUMP! THUMP!

"Ouch!" shouts Dex.

"What is it?" asks
Counselor Gus.

"My thumb has a thorn
in it!" cries Dex.

Counselor Mindy fixes his thumb.

"Thanks," says Dex.

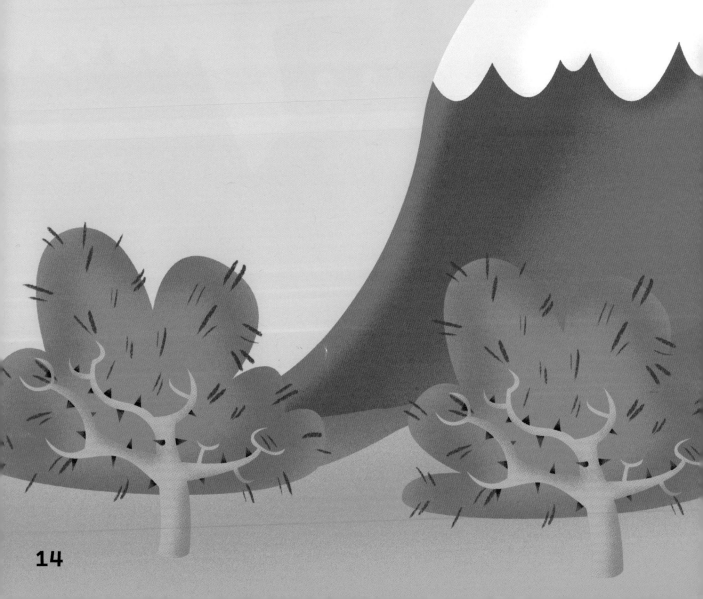

The campers hike up the mountain.

They hear a rumble.

"I think that was thunder," says Ana.

"This is not fun!" says Fitz.

Another rumble rolls through the sky.

"I know it's thunder! RUN!" shouts Counselor Gus.

The campers jump in the tram.

"This thunderstorm is scary!" screams Lizzie.

"Let's go swimming next Thursday instead," says Fitz.

After Reading Word Study

Picture Glossary

Directions: Look at each picture and read the definition. Write a list of all of the words you know that start with the same sound as *thorn*. Remember to look in the book for more words.

thermos (THUR-muhss): A thermos is a bottle that can keep liquids either hot or cold.

third (THURD): The third is after the second and before the fourth in line.

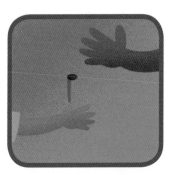 **thorn** (THORN): A thorn is a small, sharp point on a plant, usually found on the stem.

 **thrill** (THRIL): A thrill is something that gives excitement to you.

 **thumb** (THUHM): The thumb is the short, thick finger found on each hand.

 **thunder** (THUHN-dur): Thunder is the loud, rumbling sound that comes after lightning.

About the Author

Meg Greve lives in Chicago with her husband and her two kids named Madison and William. They love to go to the mountains in New Mexico. Last time, there was lots of thunder and hail too!

Ask The Author!
www.rem4students.com

About the Illustrator

Ed Myer is a Manchester-born illustrator now living in London. After growing up in an artistic household, Ed studied ceramics at university but always continued drawing pictures. As well as illustration, Ed likes traveling, playing computer games, and walking little Ted (his Jack Russell).